Z

THE ZEBRA

LYNETTE KOCH

WestBow Press books may be ordered through booksellers or by contacting:

WestBow Press
A Division of Thomas Nelson & Zondervan
1663 Liberty Drive
Bloomington, IN 47403
www.westbowpress.com
844-714-3454

ISBN: 978-1-6642-0627-4 (sc)
ISBN: 978-1-6642-0628-1 (e)

Library of Congress Control Number: 2020918352

Print information available on the last page.

WestBow Press rev. date: 10/12/2020

WESTBOW
PRESS®
A DIVISION OF THOMAS NELSON
& ZONDERVAN

Acknowlegement

To my wonderful family, especially my husband, who have shown me immeasurable support, encouragement, patience and love.

To many amazing friends who have helped to set this project in motion and have supported me with your love and kindness.

Thank you Westbow for all of your help and guiding me through the process.

Without all of you, and the promptings from God, none of this would have been possible.

I thank you with all of my heart!

May our lights shine brightly in this world to show our praise and gratitude to our Heavenly Father and to illuminate His love for this world, the one who makes all things possible.

Let your light shine!

It was an extraordinary morn in
an African meadow of green

In the tall lush grass lay and amazing
sight, one to behold and one everyone
wished they could have seen

Surrounded by family, a
newborn zebra did lay

There was something extremely
unusual about him, no one knew for
sure quite what one should say

A baby zebra was born, he was
an incredible sight to see

He had no stripes at all but polka dots of
every color, how could this possibly be

His family was in awe of this spotted
little guy and knew that he was rare

Many spots, no stripes but he was perfect
to them, they didn't seem to care

We shall call him Z and thank God
for this perfect and precious gift

Z grew quickly and was powerful,
strong and was very fast and swift

Z had spots of red, orange, yellow,
green, indigo, violet and blue

All the colors in the rainbow, how did
this happen, no one had a clue

One day little Z got angry, the
others wouldn't let him play

His red spots got even redder when
they told him to go away

He knew that he was different
and at first he didn't care

But his green spots turned even greener
when he wanted what the others
had but they didn't want to share

On bright sunny days when all was
going well and Z was having fun

His yellow spots shone like the
sunshine brighter that the sun

Z loved to race around and run to and fro

His orange spots would be all lit up,
he is so fast, you should see him go

Some days things just didn't seem to go right
and the blue spots were bluer than the sky

Z didn't really understand this
feeling, he was sad and thought
that he might even want to cry

There were days when there was a
whole lot to get done and he needed his
family and friends to work as a team

His spots of indigo would be as dark as
blueberries, he felt hopeful and at peace
when the spots were all a gleam

Most days Z would stop to think about the
world and was so thankful in his heart

His violet spots would all light up,
grateful for many things, to name
them where would he even start

Z knew these spots made him
different and that he was very rare

Some days it was fine, but when
others made fun of him, he wished
that they weren't there

Things are said that can be mean,
cruel and sometimes not very nice

His mother said, "just ignore those unkind
words, please listen and take my advice."

She told him to focus not on what
was wrong but what was right
and all the good he could do

Listen to your heart, you don't have to be
like anyone else, just be true to you.

There must be a reason that God created
you in this special way, just go about being
kind, doing good each and every day

There is a purpose to your life, there is a plan
for your future which is full of hope and love

Keep a positive attitude, God makes
no mistakes, he planned you long
ago way up in heaven above

Everyday if we are looking we
can see miracles all around

For you my dear Z are one of them,
unique, loved and perfect, as
rare as any gem ever found

Late one afternoon, the power had gone
out and soon the world would be black,
no light anywhere would be seen

Z was asked if there was anything he
could do to help, he was hoping to get his
spots to light up, any color, red, orange,
yellow, blue, violet, indigo or green

He thought and thought about what makes
his spots light up, walking to and fro

When suddenly he realized that
his spots were shining brightly
and they were all a glow

They were radiant and lit up the dark
night sky, brighter that any star

There was so much light you could
see for miles you could see real far

All the zebras were so pleased with
Z, he was their hero that night

He had something no one else had,
he could be their much needed
bright and shining light

Z was glad he had found a purpose for all
these rare spots that could be of help to all

He would come whenever they needed an
extra light or whenever they would call.

Z with his spots all a glow, every
color of the rainbow, all seven

In the same way, let your light shine
before others that they may see
your good deeds and glorify your
Father in Heaven. Matthew 5:16

CPSIA information can be obtained
at www.ICGtesting.com
Printed in the USA
BVHW020948111120
593048BV00031B/655